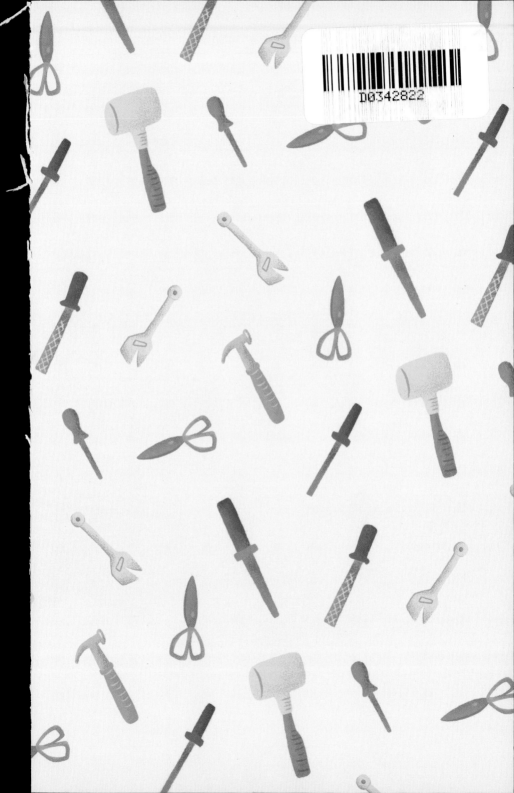

This book belongs to

Waiting for Sophie

SARAH ELLIS

Illustrated by CARMEN MOK

pajamapress

First published in Canada and the United States in 2017

The publisher gratefully acknowledges the support of the Canada Council for the Arts and the
Ontario Arts Council for its publishing program. We acknowledge the financial support of the
Government of Canada through the Canada Book Fund (CBF) for our publishing activities.

Library and Archives Canada Cataloguing in Publication

Ellis, Sarah, author
         Waiting for Sophie / Sarah Ellis ; illustrated by Carmen
Mok. – First edition.
ISBN 978-1-77278-020-8 (hardback)
         I. Mok, Carmen, illustrator II. Title.
PS8559.L57W35 2017   jC813'.54   C2016-907222-3

Publisher Cataloging-in-Publication Data (U.S.)

Names: Ellis, Sarah, 1952-, author. | Mok, Carmen, illustrator.
Title: Waiting for Sophie / Sarah Ellis ; illustrated by Carmen Mok.
Description: Toronto, Ontario, Canada : Pajama Press, 2017. | Summary: "Waiting for a
new baby is hard, and waiting for her to grow up into a playmate is even harder. Luckily
Liam's Nana is just downstairs and always ready help. When the two of them build a
Get-Older-Faster Machine, Liam is surprised to find it's not Sophie who does the most growing
up"— Provided by publisher.
Identifiers: ISBN 978-1-77278-020-8 (hardcover)
Subjects: LCSH: Babies – Juvenile fiction. | Grandmothers – Juvenile fiction. | BISAC: JUVENILE
FICTION / Readers / Intermediate. | JUVENILE FICTON / Family / New Baby.
Classification: LCC PZ7.E455Wai |DDC [E] – dc23

Manufactured by Qualibre Inc./Printplus Limited
Printed in China

Pajama Press Inc.
181 Carlaw Ave. Suite 207 Toronto, Ontario Canada, M4M 2S1

Distributed in Canada by UTP Distribution
5201 Dufferin Street Toronto, Ontario Canada, M3H 5T8

Distributed in the U.S. by Ingram Publisher Services
1 Ingram Blvd. La Vergne, TN 37086, USA

Original art created digitally
Cover and book design—Rebecca Bender

To little sisters and big brothers everywhere—S.E.

To the little one who is waiting patiently—C.M.

Chapter One

"**Liam.** Wake up!" Nana-Downstairs sat on the edge of Liam's bed.

"Big news. Baby Sophie is on her way. Mom and Dad went to the hospital."

Liam somersaulted out of bed. "Zowie! Finally! When is she coming home?"

"Maybe tomorrow."

"Tomorrow! Why so long?"

"Being born takes time. Just a bit more waiting."

"Waiting. Waiting. Waiting. I waited through half of kindergarten. I waited through my birthday." Liam bounced on the bed. "Waiting is my worst thing. I want to jump on waiting and smash it to smithereens and flush it down the toilet."

"I know," said Nana-Downstairs. "Here's an idea. Let's be bad today. There's nothing like being bad to pass the time."

Liam and Nana-Downstairs wore their pajamas all day. They even went to the corner store in their pajamas. No news of Sophie.

Liam and Nana-Downstairs did not make good nutrition choices. They ate marshmallow sandwiches for lunch. No news of Sophie.

After lunch they painted purple polka dots on the back of Liam's bedroom door. No news of Sophie.

All day long they insulted and threatened each other.

"Stinky pot pie, stinky pot pie,
Drink a pot of coffee
Or I'll poke you in the eye."
No news of Sophie.

They stayed up late watching old movies. They watched movies where the good guys and the bad guys didn't use their words. They just rode horses and beat each other up.

Then, right in the middle of a big stampede, the phone rang.

"Sophie has arrived!" said Nana-Downstairs. "Yippee ki-yay!"

Liam talked to Mom. He talked to Dad. Sophie was sleeping so he didn't talk to her.

Liam went to bed on the couch, and when he woke up in the morning, he felt happy before he remembered why. He was tired of being bad, so he got dressed and brushed his teeth. He had just started eating oatmeal when a big yellow taxi stopped in front of the house. Liam ran outside.

"She's here. She's here. She's here!" Nana-Downstairs ran around the corner from the vegetable garden.

Dad got out of the taxi and Mom got out holding a bundle that was a baby sister. Dad hugged Liam. Liam hugged Mom and the bundle. Mom and the bundle hugged Dad. Nana-Downstairs hugged Dad and Liam and Mom and the bundle. She forgot she was holding a lettuce. It got squashed and there was lettuce juice on everybody. Nobody minded.

Mom handed the bundle to Liam. "She would like you to carry her inside."

Sophie was small, but she was heavier than Liam had expected. He was very careful with his feet when he carried her through the door. He put her on the couch and unwrapped her like a present. She was practically perfect. She had toes like peanuts and ears that the sun shone through. The top of her head smelled especially nice. She smiled at Liam and held onto his finger.

Finally. A baby sister. The Big Wait was over.

Chapter Two

"**Lelefant.** Come on, Sophie, say it. Lelefant."

Liam bounced Lelefant up and down on Sophie's stomach. Sophie smiled. But she didn't say anything.

Sophie loved Liam. When Liam put socks on his ears, Sophie squeak-laughed. When Liam read books to Sophie, she paid attention to every word. Liam was the best at making Sophie stop crying and at making her burp. Liam was Sophie's favorite. Everybody said so.

But after three whole weeks, Liam was tired of burping and crying. Burping and crying and diapers and a little bit of throwing up was getting boring. It was time for Sophie to learn more things.

She was too little to sit up, but she could make noises. Why couldn't she talk?

"What's the stuffie called, Sophie? That's right, you can do it. Go for it! Say Lelefant."

Sophie said nothing.

Liam whispered, "Lelefant." He sang, "*Lelefant.*" He said, "Lelefant" in a mo-o-o-o-o-nster voice.

Sophie said nothing.

Liam shouted, "**LELEFANT**" in his outdoor voice. Dad came into the room.

"Sophie's too young to talk," said Dad. "Be patient. Sophie will grow up before you know it."

So Liam waited. He waited through the end of kindergarten and the whole of summer holidays.

"Look," said Mom. "Sophie's playing peek-a-boo."

"Look," said Dad. "Sophie's doing a push-up."

"Look," said Nana-Downstairs. "Sophie's playing the ukulele."

Sophie was not playing the ukulele. She was just bashing it.

One day Liam came home from school to find that Sophie had got hold of the paper airplane he had made. It was his best one, with a fancy design and stickers. Sophie had squished it to smithereens. It was slobbery and wrecked.

"How about some rules around here?" said Liam. "How about no wrecking my stuff?"

"Oh, Liam, I'm sorry about your airplane," said Mom. "But Sophie is too young for rules."

"How long before she grows up?" asked Liam.

"She might be walking by your birthday," said Mom.

"My birthday! That's forever away. I can't wait until my birthday!"

Liam went downstairs to visit Nana-Downstairs. She was doing downward dog. Liam did curled-up cat to ask his question.

"Does time sometimes go faster?"

Nana-Downstairs stood up and groaned a little. "It sure does. Sometimes time goes crazy-fast."

Curled-up cat is a good way to think. Liam got an idea.

"Nana-Downstairs, can you help me build something?"

"You betcha," said Nana-Downstairs. "Can you wait until tomorrow?"

"You betcha," said Liam. "I have lots of practice waiting."

Chapter Three

The next morning Liam and Nana-Downstairs met in the garage.

"Four things to know when you're building something," said Nana-Downstairs. "Thing one is measure twice, cut once." Liam nodded.

"Thing two is goggles, goggles, goggles every time." Liam nodded and put on his safety goggles.

"Thing three is righty-tighty, lefty-loosey." Liam nodded even though he did not know what that meant.

"Thing four is wear a pencil behind your ear. It makes you smart." Liam put a square yellow pencil behind his ear and felt much smarter.

"So, what's the idea?" asked Nana-Downstairs.

Liam explained his idea and Nana-Downstairs nodded. "Okay. Got it."

All day long Liam and Nana-Downstairs made the something. They sawed and hammered and nailed and glued and screwed in screws, turning right to tighten and left to loosen. Then they planed and sawed and sanded. Then they ordered pizza for lunch. Then they painted with the leftover paint from the back of Liam's door. Then they wrote the computer code to make the something work. Then they cleaned up.

By supper time it was finished. It was beautiful—bright shiny purple with dials and screens and switches and wires and a keyboard and glued-on fancy pasta. Above the small door was a large sign: The G.O.F. machine.

Everybody came to look: Mom, Dad, Sophie, and the cat from next door.

"What does G.O.F. mean?" asked Dad.

"Get Older Faster," said Liam. "It makes time speed up."

"Let me guess," said Mom. "You're going to make Sophie older faster?"

"You betcha!" said Liam.

"When?" said Dad.

"Right now," said Liam. "I can't wait."

"Just a minute," said Nana-Downstairs. "I want to check we didn't leave any nails around." She crawled inside the machine.

"Ooof!"

"What's wrong?" said Mom.

"Oh, phooey, I twisted my knee," said a voice from inside the G.O.F. machine.

Dad helped Nana-Downstairs back through the little door and got her a chair to sit on.

"Hey, Liam," said Nana-Downstairs. "It works! The machine made me older faster."

"Oh, Nana," said Liam. "That's silly. It wasn't even turned on."

Liam collected everything he needed: three cushions, a binky, Lelefant, and one baby sister.

Mom and Dad looked worried.

"I like Sophie the way she is," said Dad.

"She isn't going to turn into a teenager, is she?" asked Mom. "I'm not ready for a teenager."

Nana-Downstairs did not look worried. "Go for it, Soph!"

Liam arranged Sophie on the cushions. He stuck the binky in her mouth and tucked Lelefant beside her and gave her a high-five. He backed out of the G.O.F. machine and quietly closed the door. Then he typed in a secret password, booted up the G.O.F. machine, dialed some dials, switched some switches, and keyed some keys. There was a low hum, and then...

"Waaaaaaaaaa!"

Oh no! Something had happened to Sophie!

Liam dived into the machine. Sophie was practically upside down. She had fallen off the cushions and lost her binky. Inside the G.O.F. machine, the crying was very loud.

Outside the G.O.F. machine, Sophie kept on crying. Mom tried to soothe her. Dad tried to soothe her. Nana-Downstairs tried to soothe her. Sophie cried on.

"See what you can do, Liam," said Mom. "You're the best at making Sophie stop crying."

Liam sat on the ground and hugged and rocked her.

"Hush, little baby, don't cry a bit.
Liam's gonna make you a banana split.
If that banana split tastes yucky,
Liam's gonna to buy you a garbage trucky.
If that garbage trucky gets stinky..."

Sophie stopped crying. Then she hiccupped. Then she squeak-laughed.

Nana-Downstairs turned off the G.O.F. machine.

"Do you think it worked?" said Liam.

"Try a test," said Nana-Downstairs.

Liam turned Sophie around to face him.

"Okay, Sophie. Say banana. Go on, say it. Ba. Na. Na. You can do it!"

"So-phie, So-phie!" Nana-Downstairs was acting like a cheerleader.

Sophie looked at Liam. She didn't say banana. She didn't even say ba. She grabbed Liam's ear. She held on tight.

"It didn't work," said Liam.

"That's too bad," said Mom. "But you did build something amazing." Mom and Dad took Sophie inside for her nap.

Nana-Downstairs limped over to the G.O.F. machine and pulled out Lelefant. Some of his insides were leaking out.

"I remember when Lelefant was new. When you were a baby. He looks a lot older. He even looks older than he did this morning. Maybe the G.O.F. machine only works on stuffies and grandmothers."

"Maybe," said Liam.

"Are you disappointed?"

"Yes," said Liam. "The G.O.F. machine is just junk. I want to smash it to smithereens and flush it down the toilet."

"Your decision," said Nana-Downstairs. "But I'd like to keep it for myself for a few days. Okay with you?"

"I guess," said Liam.

"Want to help me wash the car?"

Liam did not feel like washing the car.

"Would long spaghetti make you feel better? There's nothing like long spaghetti when you're down in the dumps."

"Maybe," said Liam.

Chapter Four

Two weeks later, The G.O.F. machine was still in the yard. Not smashed to smithereens. Nana-Downstairs painted over the sign.

"Let's keep it," she said. "It will make a good clubhouse. Now that you are in grade one, you will probably need a clubhouse. Clubs are what kids do in grade one."

One Saturday morning, just before Halloween, Mom said that it was girls' day out.

"Nana-Downstairs and Sophie and I are going out for a mani-pedi and lunch."

"Good," said Dad. "I'm going to buy a change table for Sophie and put it together."

Mom looked at Nana-Downstairs. Nana-Downstairs looked at Mom.

"Is that a good idea?" said Mom. "You don't really like doing Do-It-Yourself yourself."

"How hard can it be?" asked Dad.

As Nana-Downstairs left, she whispered to Liam, "Do you know where the Band-Aids are?"

Liam nodded.

"Okay. Just make sure he doesn't re-drill."

Liam nodded again. But he didn't know what re-drill meant.

Dad and Liam brought home the change table in flat boxes. They unpacked it and arranged all the pieces on the floor. There were a lot of pieces.

"Goggles," said Liam. "Goggles every time."

"Where are the directions?" asked Dad. "Oh no! There are no words, just pictures. Oh well, how hard can it be?"

It can be very hard to put together a Do-It-Yourself change table yourself.

"What is this do-ma-hickey for?" said Dad. "It doesn't look like anything in the picture."

"I might have this piece backward," said Dad.

"There's something missing," said Dad. "There is definitely something missing."

Dad dropped a hammer on his foot. He hopped around on his other foot. He started to use his outdoor voice.

"Why won't these pancake-flippin' screws go in?" said Dad. "I think the holes are in the wrong place. I'm going to re-drill."

"No, no!" yelled Liam. "Whatever you do, don't re-drill!"

Dad sat down on the floor and put his head in his hands.

"Let me see," said Liam. He tucked a pencil behind his ear. He picked up the screws. "I have an idea."

Liam went into the bathroom and scraped the screws across a bar of soap.

"Try it now."

Dad put one screw in a hole and turned the screwdriver round and round. Righty-tighty.

"Liam," he said in a calm, indoor voice. "These go in like butter! How did you know that trick?"

"Nana-Downstairs taught me," said Liam. "She said I was a natural."

When the girls got home, the change table was perfect. Everyone celebrated with doughnuts. Dad told the story of doing Do-It-Yourself himself. "But I would never have done it without Liam. He saved me."

"Liam can be the family Do-It-Yourselfer from now on," said Nana-Downstairs.

Mom gave Liam a big hug. "How did you grow up in such a hurry?"

Liam looked out the window at the purple clubhouse, formerly known as the

Get Older Faster machine. He thought about diving in to rescue Sophie. Diving in when the machine was still turned on. He was only in there about a minute. How long did it take to get older faster?

He gave Sophie a little piece of doughnut. Her face was covered in powdered sugar.

"Liam," she said, clear as a bell.

31901060681188